The Good Ship Crocodile

J. Patrick Lewis & Monique Felix

Creative Editions

Snout lived i

wee ly home on a big river.

During the wet, rainy season

Snout watched the river rise.

begged Sparkle, the brightest glimmer-glow

by. "Please carry us to the other side,"

of all. "We cannot fly in this rain."

So

they went.

In the days that followed, other neighbors asked to be carried across the big river.

Finally, the sun gulped up all the wate

Snout had drifted far down the river.

Now the weary crocodile could not see

As night fell

his home.

so did Snout's spirits.

Just then a firefly danced by

"Sparkle," Snout cried, "I am lost!"

Sparkle blinked a

blink to all her sisters.

They set off in the dark across

the dry land, Snout in tow.

By firefly light, the Good Ship

Crocodile found his way home.

Text copyright © 2013 J. Patrick Lewis
Illustrations copyright © 2013 Monique Felix
Published in 2013 by Creative Editions
P.O. Box 227, Mankato, MN 56002 USA
Creative Editions is an imprint of The Creative Company.
Designed by Rita Marshall. Edited by Aaron Frisch.

Library of Congress Cataloging-in-Publication Data
Lewis, J. Patrick.
The Good Ship Crocodile / by J. Patrick Lewis; illustrated by Monique Felix.
Summary: During the rainy season, when the river rises,
Snout the crocodile helps many creatures cross to the other side,
but when the rain stops and the river dries up,
it is Snout who needs help getting home.
ISBN 978-1-56846-238-7
[1. Crocodiles—Fiction. 2. Animals—Fiction.
3. Rain and rainfall—Fiction.] I. Félix, Monique, illustrator. II. Title.
PZ7.L5866Goo 2013   [E]—dc23   2012051781
2 4 6 8 9 7 5 3